POLICEMAN
SMALL

LOIS LENSKI

Random House 🏠 New York

OH, DO YOU KNOW POLICEMAN SMALL?

WORDS BY LOIS LENSKI
MUSIC BY CLYDE ROBERT BULLA

Policeman Small is a traffic cop.
    He stands at the street crossing.
He wears white gloves. He tells
the cars when to go and stop.

It is six o'clock in the morning.
Here comes the milk delivery truck.
"Hello, Joe!" calls Policeman
Small. "Has everybody got milk
for breakfast?"
"Yes!" says Joe.

It is eight-thirty.

Here come the schoolchildren walking to school.

Policeman Small holds up his hand. The children cross the street.

They say, "Hello, Policeman Small!"

It is nine o'clock.

Here comes a farmer in a truck. He has a load of vegetables for the grocery store. He waves to Policeman Small.

It is ten o'clock.

Here comes a sports car very fast.

It comes faster and faster. It is speeding.

Policeman Small blows his whistle very loud. He holds up his hand.

The car stops. Policeman Small
runs up. "No speeding here, sir!" he
says. "25 miles an hour in town!"
"Sorry!" says the young man.
He drives on.

It is ten-thirty.

A siren sounds. It goes on and on. Here comes an ambulance. It is going to the hospital. Somebody is sick.

Policeman Small clears the street. The ambulance goes whizzing by.

It is eleven o'clock. Here comes a circus parade. The band is playing. Policeman Small is on his motorcycle. He rides in front to lead the way.

It is eleven-thirty.

The parade is over. Policeman Small shoos the people back to the sidewalk. A little boy is lost. He cries and cries.

Policeman Small finds his mother for him.

It is twelve o'clock.

Here comes another farm truck. It has milk cans in the back. It goes *rattledy-bang!* A milk can falls off. The milk spills on the street.

Tweet-tweet-tweet! Policeman Small blows his whistle.

The farmer stops his truck.

"Sorry!" he says.

"Too bad!" says Policeman Small.

They pick up the milk can and put it on the truck. The truck goes on to the dairy.

Policeman Small holds up
his hand. Two cats are licking up
the spilled milk. They are hungry.
The cars must wait.

Twelve-thirty. It is lunchtime.
Policeman Small goes to a drugstore.
   He eats two sandwiches. He has
ice cream and coffee. He takes a
little rest.

Now it is afternoon. Traffic is heavy.
Policeman Small brings his Stop–Go sign.

Cars and trucks come rolling by. Big
cars and little cars. Big trucks and little
trucks. A boy on a bicycle.

Policeman Small turns on "Go."

They all go.

It is one-thirty.

Policeman Small turns on "Stop."

The cars stop. All the people cross. A little dog stops in the middle of the street.

Policeman Small picks him up. He puts him on the sidewalk. Now he is safe.

The cars can go again.

It is two o'clock.

Bang, bangety, bump! A big truck bumps into the back of a little car.

Policeman Small runs over.

"Hey!" he calls. "Pull up by the curb."

"His brakes are not good!" says the man in the little car.

"He stopped too soon!" says the man in the truck.

Policeman Small writes down their names and license numbers. He gives them tickets. He sends them to the police station to talk it over.

It is three o'clock.

The two men come out of the police station.

"We have settled it. He will pay for the damage and fix his brakes," says the man in the little car.

"Good!" says Policeman Small.

The men drive off.

It is four o'clock.

R-r-r-r-r! A school bus goes rolling by. It is full of children. They are going home from school.

They wave to Policeman Small.

It is five o'clock.

A siren sounds. It goes on and on.

Policeman Small blows his whistle three times. He holds out both his arms. He clears the street.

A fire engine goes whizzing by. It is going to a fire. All the people look.

Now it is gone.
Policeman Small turns on "Go."
The cars can go again. They are
all going home. It is getting late.

It is six o'clock.

"Whew!" says Policeman Small. "Big day today! Now I can go home!"

He picks up his Stop–Go sign and goes.

His day is over.

*And that's all
about
Policeman Small!*